W9-AMP-958

-My Family-
My Two Homes

by Claudia Harrington
illustrated by Zoe Persico

Looking Glass Library

An Imprint of Magic Wagon
abdopublishing.com

To my amazing family, who make me smile. —CH

To my wonderful Papa for always being such a great inspiration and making me smile. —ZP

abdopublishing.com

Published by Magic Wagon, a division of ABDO, PO Box 398166, Minneapolis, Minnesota 55439. Copyright © 2016 by Abdo Consulting Group, Inc. International copyrights reserved in all countries. No part of this book may be reproduced in any form without written permission from the publisher. Looking Glass Library™ is a trademark and logo of Magic Wagon.

Printed in the United States of America, North Mankato, Minnesota.
052015
092015

 THIS BOOK CONTAINS RECYCLED MATERIALS

Written by Claudia Harrington
Illustrated by Zoe Persico
Edited by Heidi M.D. Elston
Designed by Candice Keimig

Library of Congress Cataloging-in-Publication Data

Harrington, Claudia, 1957- author.
  My two homes / by Claudia Harrington ; illustrated by Zoe Persico.
     pages cm. -- (My family)
  Summary: Lenny follows Skye for a school project and learns about her life with two homes.
  ISBN 978-1-62402-109-1
1. Children of divorced parents--Juvenile fiction. 2. Parent and child--Juvenile fiction. 3. Families--Juvenile fiction. [1. Divorce--Fiction. 2. Parent and child--Fiction. 3. Family life--Fiction. 4. Youths' art.] I. Persico, Zoe, 1993- illustrator. II. Title.
  PZ7.1.H374Mv 2016
  [E]--dc23
                                    2015002677

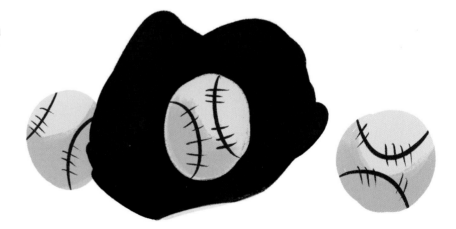

When the school day was over, Miss Fish handed Lenny the class camera. "You're heading home with Skye today, Lenny. She's Student of the Week."

"Hi," said Skye.

"Hi, Skye! Do you take the bus?" asked Lenny.
Click!

"No, I live close," said Skye. She tossed a baseball as they walked.
"Do you like baseball?" asked Lenny.

"You could say that." Skye ran ahead and threw him a fastball. *Whoosh!* Lenny caught the ball before it hit the camera.

"Wow! You're good," said Skye.

Lenny rubbed his hand. "Thanks."

Skye led Lenny into the lobby
of a tall building. "Home sweet
home, part one," she said.
"Part one?" asked Lenny. **Click!**

"This is Dad's place," said Skye. When they got in the elevator, she pushed 3.

"Dad!" called Skye. "Come meet
Lenny. He's a great catcher!"
Skye tumbled into her dad.
Click!

Skye blushed. "Sorry, Dad."

Her dad laughed. "Skye, the human fastball! Why don't you two grab a snack, then pitch yourselves into homework?"

"We only have to read one chapter tonight," said Skye, tossing Lenny some peanuts. "Want to see my room?"

"Sure," said Lenny.

"Cool! Who decorated it?"
Click!
"Dad did this one," Skye said.
"Go, Sox!" yelled her dad.

"Who plays catch with you?" asked Lenny.

"All my parents," said Skye. "But since you're here, you can!"

"Homework first," called her dad.

"Dad hears like a bat," said Skye.

When they finished reading, Skye tossed a catcher's mitt to Lenny and led him to the park.

Whoosh!

"Who taught you how to pitch a fastball?" asked Lenny.

"My mom," said Skye.

Sweeeeesh!

Lenny grinned. "Did she teach you that wicked curve ball, too?"

"That'd be my dad," said Skye.

Flawoosh!

Lenny laughed. "And that knuckleball?"

"Nick's favorite," said Skye. "He's my stepdad.
Now, for my mystery pitch!"

"Wait!" said Lenny. **Click!**

Fwooot!

The ball flew right into his glove.

"Wow! Great slider!"

19

Skye's dad arrived. "Dinner's ready!"
"Does your dad always make your dinner?"
asked Lenny.
"When I'm here.
Mom does the rest
of the time."

"But I'm the best cook." Her dad winked.
"He really is," whispered Skye. "But don't
tell my mom!"

Bzzzzzt!

"Skye, it's your mom and Nick," said her dad. **Click!**

"Hug!" said Skye's mom.

"You have three parents?" asked Lenny.

Skye nodded.

"Who loves you best?" asked Lenny.

"We all do!" said Skye's parents.

"See you tomorrow, sweetie," said her dad.

"Bye, Dad," said Skye.

Click!

"Home sweet home, part two," said Skye. **Click!**

"Anyone still hungry?" asked Skye's mom.

"Nope, we're full," said Skye.

"That's too bad," said her mom.

"I'm the better cook!"

Skye and Lenny shared a grin.

Click!

"Come see my room!" said Skye.

"Wow," said Lenny. "You have two of everything! Who painted this room?" **Click!**

Skye smiled. "Nick did."

"Bedtime soon," said Nick.

"Do you have a night-light?" asked Lenny.

"Over there," pointed Skye.

"Oooh! Mine's not nearly that cool!" said Lenny. "Who reads your bedtime story?"

"My turn tonight," said Skye's mom.

Dingdong!

"Your mom is here, Lenny," called Skye's mom.

"Not already!" said Lenny.

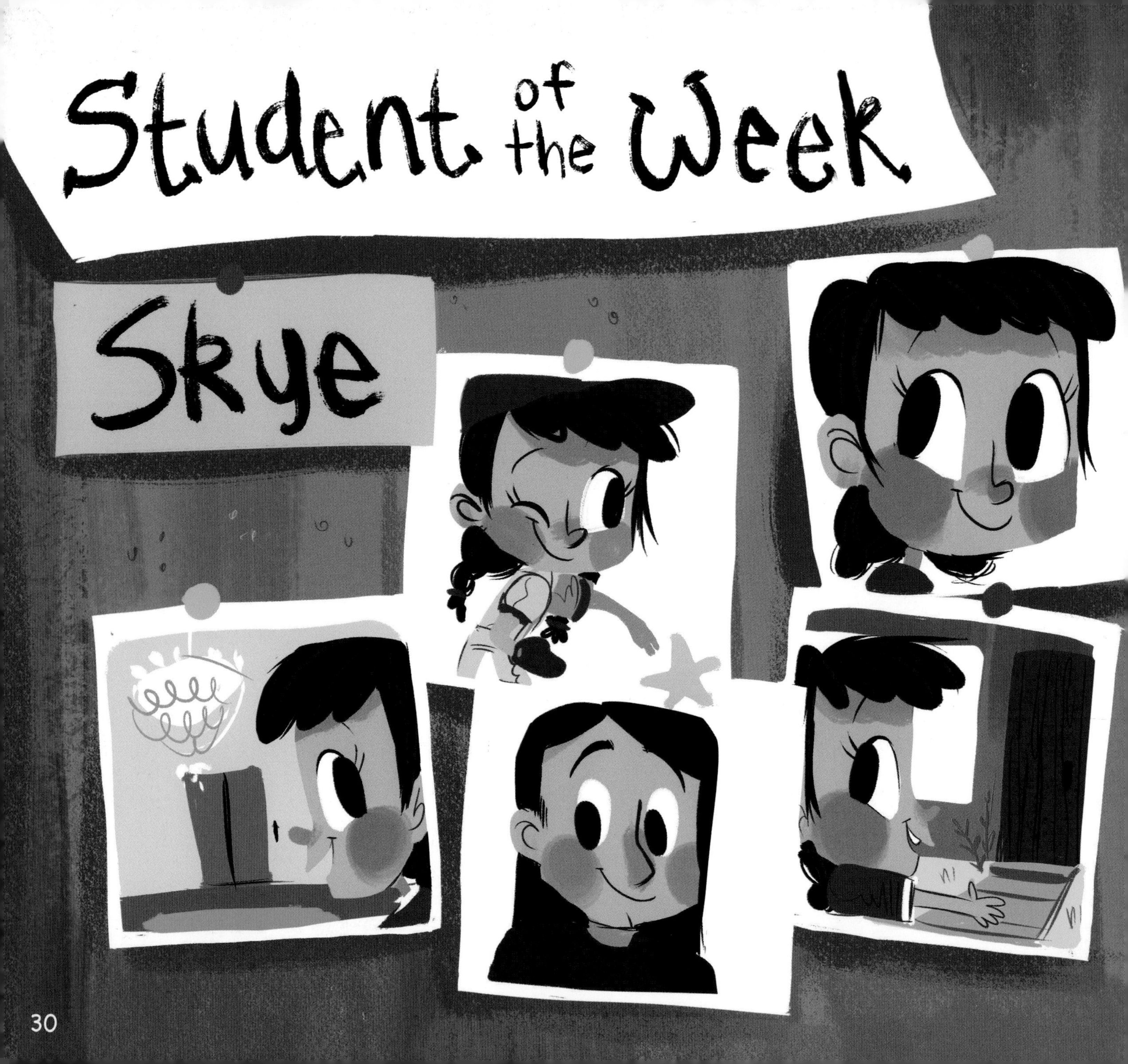
Student of the Week
Skye

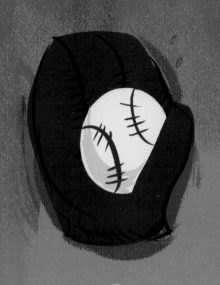

"See you at school, Hall of Famer!"
said Lenny.
Skye waved. "Catch you later!"